Race of a Lifetime

Tony Norman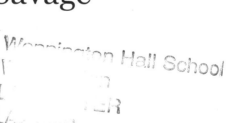

Illustrated by
Paul Savage

D0185330

 FULL FLIGHT

Titles in Full Flight

Badger Publishing Limited
26 Wedgwood Way, Pin Green Industrial Estate, Stevenage,
Hertfordshire SG1 4QF
Telephone: 01438 356907. Fax: 01438 747015.
www.badger-publishing.co.uk   enquiries@badger-publishing.co.uk

Race of a Lifetime   ISBN 1 85880 926 6

Text © Tony Norman 2002
Series editing © Jonny Zucker 2002
Complete work © Badger Publishing Limited 2002

Series Editor: Jonny Zucker.
Publisher: David Jamieson.
Editor: Paul Martin.
Cover design: Jain Birchenough.
Cover illustration: Paul Savage.

Race of a
Lifetime

Tony Norman

Illustrated by
Paul Savage

Contents

Badger Publishing

Chapter 1 - The Dream

Jamie could see the finishing line.

High above him, at the top of a steep, muddy hill.

There was so much noise, Jamie couldn't think. Teachers, parents and kids from school, all staring at him. He felt the sweat run down his face.

Jamie was pumping the pedals of his bike like crazy, but he felt like he was stuck in one spot.

"What is this?" he kept asking himself. "What's going wrong?"

Then he heard a loud voice, through a speaker.

"And here's Jamie Collins, riding the oldest bike in the race. Better late than never, Jamie!"

The truth hit Jamie like a smack in the face. The people on the hill weren't cheering. They were laughing. Laughing at him and his stupid old bike.

Jamie felt a burst of anger deep inside.

He pedalled faster and faster.

He had just one thought in his mind.

Must finish the race. Must finish the race. Must finish the...

"Oi! Look out!"

Jamie swerved and slid to a stop.

"You want to be more careful, son."

The milkman looked angry.

Jamie stared at him. A milkman? What was he doing here?

Then Jamie's mind jumped back to the real world. Back to Friday morning. Back to his paper round.

Now he understood... the laughing faces were just in his mind.

"Sorry," said Jamie. "I was... just..."

"Daydreaming!" said the milkman. He climbed into his milk float and drove off.

Jamie felt angry. He jumped off his old bike and kicked it.

"Heap of old junk," he shouted. Then he kicked the bike again.

What chance did he have in the school race on that old thing?

Jamie's mind was made up. He knew what he must do.

Chapter 2 - Buzzing

When Jamie got home, he tried to talk
to his dad. It wasn't easy. The kitchen
was full of people.

Jamie was 13. He had two sisters and
two brothers, all younger than him.
This morning, like every morning, he
felt like they all came from another
planet.

Jamie's youngest sister was called Sharon. She was nine, but seemed older. She sat on her own at the computer.

Jamie's mum kept giving time checks, like a DJ on the radio.

"Come on you lot, it's ten to eight," she shouted above the din.

Jamie's dad was playing his guitar. The sound of his voice made Jamie think of stray cats howling in the dead of night. When dad stopped for a bite of toast, Jamie took his chance.

"I want a mountain bike for the school race," he said.

"Who's going to pay for it?" dad asked.

"Me, I've been saving up from my paper round."

"Well, sure then, that's cool," dad smiled. "Nice one, Jamie. Go for it!"

Jamie hated it when his dad tried to sound cool, but this time it didn't matter.

Jamie was buzzing inside.

Chapter 3 - s-zone

That night, Jamie went on the Internet to find out how much a mountain bike would cost. Every website gave him the same bad news. Jamie hardly had the cash to buy a new wheel, let alone a new bike.

"Don't stay on there too long," called his mum.

Jamie didn't argue. He logged off the Internet and checked his e-mails. There was one message in his Inbox.

Jamie

From: s-zone

To: Jamie Collins

Date: 8 April

Subject: Top Bike

Hi Jamie

See local paper. For Sale. Page 16. Do it now.

s-zone

Jamie sat back and stared at the screen. He had no idea who the e-mail was from, but he decided to check it out.

He found the local paper. He saw the ad for the second-hand bike. He made the call. He spoke to the boy who was selling.

First thing next morning, Jamie saw the bike. It was a bit rusty and had lots of dents and scratches.

That didn't faze him. The main thing was, the bike was cheap; a price Jamie could afford. So, he bought it.

Jamie was happy, but he still kept asking himself the same question.

Who is s-zone?

Chapter 4 - Selfish

The big race was just two weeks away. There were posters all over school.

When Jamie thought about the race, his heart beat faster. He must get his bike ready in time. He spent every spare minute working on it, in the garden shed.

Sharon, his kid sister, started hanging round. At first, she got on Jamie's nerves, but he soon saw she could be useful.

Sharon didn't seem to mind what she did, as long as Jamie let her help.

They both worked hard.

Jamie took the bike apart. He worked on the frame. The dents and scratches were small. He soon fixed them. Then he painted the frame jet black. It looked really cool.

Sharon washed the mud off the tyres. She found they were as good as new.

Then she got all the rust off the wheels and painted them silver.

One week later, Jamie's bike was ready to ride.

His mum said they must go to the local bike shop first, for a safety check. Mum paid, so Jamie didn't mind.

The man in the shop checked the brakes and the 6-speed gear change. He said the bike was fine. Jamie's mum bought him a helmet, elbow-pads and knee-pads. Jamie put them on. Sharon said he looked good, but Jamie wasn't listening.

Before they left, the man set the saddle to just the right height for Jamie.

Now the bike was perfect and Jamie was on top of the world.

"Can I try your bike later?" said Sharon. Her voice was small and timid.

"No you can't!" snapped Jamie. "Try my bike, now it's all set up for the race? Are you crazy?"

Sharon didn't say a word, but her face went red.

"Jamie," said his mum, in a hurt voice, "... after all Sharon's done for you."

Jamie left his mum and Sharon at the shop.

The bike was great, but Jamie felt sick inside. He kept seeing Sharon's sad face. Why had he shouted at her like that?

"Collins, you're a selfish rat!" he said out loud and pedalled harder and faster, all the way home.

One hour later, Sharon's mum's mobile beeped. She read the text message.

"I think this is for you, love."

"What does it say?" asked Sharon.
"You read it," said mum, handing her
the phone.

The message was short and sweet :

```
ur my coach ok?
```

Sharon knew who the text was from...

Chapter 5 - Go For It!

Jamie knew he'd been mean to Sharon. He wanted to make up for it now.

But did he really want her to be his coach? No, of course not.

The way Jamie saw it, he'd do some training for the 'Race of a Lifetime' and Sharon could come and watch, simple as that.

But Sharon had other ideas. They did not have long to train, so she'd make sure Jamie worked... very hard indeed!

Training started on Monday, after
school. Jamie had a map of where the
bikes would race on the common. He
did a test lap round the track.

"Do it again," said Sharon. "This time,
when you get to that last hill... go for it!"

Jamie looked at Sharon. She was a tough coach, but what she said made sense.

So, he got back on his bike and tried again.

Tuesday. Wednesday. Thursday. Every training session was better than the last.

"Nice one!" smiled Sharon, after the last lap on Thursday. "Best time yet, by nine seconds. You can win this race Jamie... you can really win it!"

"I still hate that hill," said Jamie.

"We'll sort it out," said Sharon. "Nothing can stop us now."

But she was wrong!

Chapter 6 - Nightmare

Friday morning. 7.34 a.m.

That's when Jamie's world caved in.

He came out of a block of flats on his paper round and stared round in horror.

His bike had been stolen. This couldn't be happening, but it was.

The rest of Friday was like a bad dream.

Sharon helped Jamie look for his bike. They searched all over town. They asked every kid they met, but nobody knew a thing. It was hopeless.

Jamie felt so bad, he didn't want to get up on Saturday.

Sharon told him he was a wimp and he knew she was right, so they went to watch the race together. Suddenly, Sharon ran off through the crowd.

"That's my brother's bike, you thief!"

Sharon was shouting at a sly-looking
boy, twice her size.

She tried to take the bike, but the boy
pushed her away. Jamie didn't like
that.

He grabbed the bike from the boy and gave him a hard look. The boy's dad stormed up to them.

"What's going on?" he shouted.

Sharon wasn't afraid. She turned the bike upside down and pointed to some silver letters painted under the saddle. They read: s-zone.

"That's my e-mail name," said Sharon. "Ask my mum if you don't believe me. I put it there for luck, when I helped Jamie paint this bike. Your son stole it."

The sly boy went red. His dad dragged him away, without another word. Jamie was in shock.

"You're s-zone?" he said to Sharon. "I didn't... I mean... You're s-zone?"

"Better get over it, Jamie," Sharon grinned. "You're back in the race!"

Chapter 7 - Winner or Loser?

The race flew past in a blur. Jamie was a blaze of energy. Down the hill, he rushed. Over the bridge and back across the small stream. His legs felt strong as he pedalled fast across the long, flat field beside the line of trees.

The race was nearly over and Jamie was in the lead. He could see the finishing line high above him, at the top of the steep muddy hill. Now, for the final test! Jamie stood up and pedalled as hard as he could go.

The noise of the crowd filled his ears. But were they cheering, or laughing at him, like in his dream ?

Don't think about it, he told himself, but it was too late. Another bike zipped into the lead. Mud from its wheels flew up in his face. Jamie knew he had lost.

The rider in the lead was just metres from the line. He put one hand in the air and waved to the crowd. Then his foot slipped from a muddy pedal. His bike twisted to the right and Jamie was past him and over the line in a flash.

Jamie couldn't believe it. He'd won!

"... so folks, let's hear it for our 'Race of a Lifetime' champion, Jamie Collins!"

"Hold the Cup up, Jamie," yelled the photographer from the local paper. Jamie saw Sharon in the crowd.

"Come on!" he yelled above the cheers.

Posing for the photos felt good, like being a star or something. Sharon held one side of the Cup and Jamie held the other.

There were smiling faces all around. Then Jamie gave Sharon a present. It was his gold medal for winning the race.

"It's yours," smiled Jamie. "Couldn't have won it without you... coach!"